CHRISTOPHER REEVE

CHRISTOPHER REEVE

Triumph over Tragedy
by Judy Alter

A Book Report Biography
FRANKLIN WATTS
A Division of Grolier Publishing
New York / London / Hong Kong / Sydney
Danbury, Connecticut

Frontispiece: Christopher Reeve with his wife Dana
and daughter Alexandra

Cover illustration by Dave Klaboe, interpreted from a photograph
by © AP/Wide World Photos/Eric Draper

Photographs ©: AP/Wide World Photos: cover, 77 (Eric Draper), 29
(Daniel Hulshizer); Archive Photos: 81 (Kosta Alexander/Fotos
International), 94 (Dave Allocca/Reuters), 51 (Express Newspapers), 73
(Fotos International), 53 (Lambert), 63 (Sonia Moskowitz), 98 (Jeff
Neira/Reuters), 92 (Ron Sachs/CNP); Corbis-Bettmann: 9 (David Allen), 23
(Paul Almasy), 46 (UPI), 65; Liaison Agency, Inc.: 2, 85 (Agostini), 67, 71
(Steve Allen), 88 (Jonathan Elderfield), 12 (Loren Fisher), 70 (Gifford), 19
(Stephanie Gross/The Daily Progress), 74 (King), 96 (Lawrence
Schwartzwald), 69 (Uzzle); Photofest: 58 (Cannon Films Inc./
Warner Bros. Inc./DC Comics Inc.), 33, 39, 41, 43, 49, 57.

Visit Franklin Watts on the Internet at:
http://publishing.grolier.com

Library of Congress Cataloging-in-Publication Data

Alter, Judy, 1938–
Christopher Reeve: triumph over tragedy / by Judy Alter
    p. cm. – (Book report biography)
Includes bibliographical references and index.
    Summary: A biography of the actor famous for playing Superman, dis-
cussing his activities before and after the accident that paralyzed him as
well as his work as an activist for environmental causes, artistic and
human rights, and disability rights.
ISBN 0-531-11674-3 (lib. bdg.) 0-531-16455-1 (pbk.)
    1. Reeve, Christopher, 1952—Juvenile literature. 2. Actors—United
States—Biography—Juvenile literature. 3. Quadriplegics—United
States—Biography—Juvenile literature. [1. Reeve, Christopher, 1952– 2.
Actors and actresses. 3. Quadriplegics. 4. Physically handicapped.] I. Title.
II. Series.

PN2287.R292 A48   2000
791.43'028'092—dc21
[B]   99-087463

CONTENTS

CHAPTER ONE

REEVE FACES TRAGEDY

Christopher Reeve has done more than meet tragedy straight on and rise above it. Once a movie superstar and now a quadriplegic, he has emerged from a devastating accident with a strong voice that speaks for the handicapped and disabled. From a wheelchair and a respirator, he has used his reputation as an activist and his connection with influential people to become America's most powerful spokesman for research into spinal cord injury. His activism goes beyond the pain suffered by the quadriplegic and such issues of accessibility as wider doors and ramps. Reeve also fights to stop insurance companies from setting lifetime limits on benefits for patients with spinal cord injury. He has called for the federal government to spend as much on spinal cord research as it spends on the military. Christopher Reeve is among the most admired Americans today. One person we might compare him with is one of Reeve's own personal heroes—the wheelchair-bound President Franklin Delano Roosevelt, who guided the United States for twelve years.

In 1995, Christopher Reeve was a man to be envied. An actor with a long list of film and stage credits, he was best known for his lead roles in the four Superman movies. By the 1990s, after a brief career slump, he was moving into more complex and mature roles and, after several years of television and stage work, was once again receiving lucrative movie offers.

The father of two teen-aged children from a previous relationship, he was married to the former Dana Morosini, whom he called his "life force" and credited with helping him grow into a mature, responsible person. The couple had a two-year-old son, Will, and homes in Williamstown, Massachusetts, and Westchester County, New York. Reeve had become politically active as a spokesman for environmental issues and the National Endowment for the Arts. He was also a founding member of The Creative Coalition, a group of artists who speak out for the homeless. He supported such causes as international human rights, preservation of historic theaters, served as an advisor to the American Medical Association

Christopher Reeve and his wife Dana

council on alcoholism, publicly supported AIDS research, and gave generously to many charities.

Beyond acting, Reeve had many interests. His favorite activities included flying, skiing, tennis, sailing, mountain-climbing, parasailing—whatever was "on the edge." He owned a turboprop airplane and often flew solo across the Atlantic Ocean.

He had survived several accidents, including a 1984 parasailing incident in which he unknowingly used equipment that was not strong enough to hold a man of his size and weight. All four straps slipped through the buckles, and Reeve fell 90 feet (27.5 meters) into about 4 feet (1.2 m) of water. He had the presence of mind to curl up in a ball and hit the water sideways, and suffered nothing more than a bad bruise. He had also broken an ankle while skiing, bruised ribs while playing hockey, contracted malaria, and recovered from an emergency appendectomy in one day. Christopher Reeve had not only survived a number of accidents but overcame them quickly.

He had never been injured in his most dangerous sport—jumping horses. Reeve was a superb and dedicated horseman. He first became interested in riding while filming *Anna Karenina* in Hungary in 1984. He wanted to do his own riding in his role as Vronsky, a cavalry captain in the film, so he took antihistamines—he had been allergic to horses as a child—and began lessons. Other riders in the cast were members of the Hungarian equestrian team, and one day Reeve rode in a 19th-century version of a steeplechase race with them. The experience was so exhilarating that he decided to get serious about riding.

Reeve rode often. Wherever he was filming, he found the best trainer in the area and took lessons. By the late 1980s he was competing in equestrian events. Sometimes he had to forgo this pleasure, however, because many of his movie contracts contained a "no jumping" clause. During the filming of *The Black Fox*, a CBS miniseries completed just before his accident, Reeve played a cowboy and was in the saddle for days at a time, doing his own stunts. Director Robert Halmi, Sr., told *People* magazine that Reeve was always in total control.

In May 1995, he wanted to compete once more before leaving for Ireland to film *Kidnapped,* director Francis Ford Coppola's version of the famous novel by Robert Louis Stevenson.

THE ACCIDENT

Then on May 27, 1995, during the horse trials of the Commonwealth Dressage and Combined Training Association—a three-day competition in precision horsemanship in Culpeper County, Vir-

Reeve at an equestrian event a year before the accident

ginia—Reeve's life changed dramatically and permanently. He was riding Eastern Express, a chestnut-colored American thoroughbred he called Buck, in a jumping event in which the horse and rider must jump over ditches, hedges, and fences. Riding looks effortless but requires great physical and mental control as well as endless hours of practice. Two weeks earlier, he had ridden Buck in an event where he "ate the course up." The horse was talented and seemed to enjoy competition.

At first Reeve intended to ride in a Vermont event that Memorial Day weekend, but several riders at the stable where he kept his horse had decided to go to Culpeper and persuaded him to go along. He arrived the day before and walked over the course many times, looking for dips in the ground, shadows, anything that might spook his horse. He wanted to be thoroughly familiar with the course. In the morning race that Saturday, he finished fourth out of twenty-seven competitors.

Reeve now has no memory from his arrival at the stables that afternoon until he regained consciousness several days later in the intensive care unit (ICU) at the hospital. Witnesses have told him that he and Buck sailed over the first two of fifteen jumps and headed for the third, a relatively easy 3-foot (30-centimeter) rail jump. Suddenly something went terribly wrong. Buck put his front feet over the fence, but his hind feet never left the ground. Reeve, who had already committed his large body to following the horse over the jump, flew over the animal's head. Nobody will ever know what caused the accident—Reeve thinks he may have shifted a little too far forward and the horse felt his weight move. Some people say a rabbit may have spooked Buck. Others suggest Buck simply chickened out. But Buck had never stopped on a cross-country course before, so it was unbelievable that he stopped before a fence so low that he could almost have walked over it. Reeve does not dwell on whether his horse saw a rabbit or shadows. He believes that he must personally accept responsibility for the accident.

For whatever reason, the horse backed off the jump. Pushed by his own momentum, Reeve kept going, flying forward over the horse's neck. Buck, perhaps out of instinct, had lowered his head, in effect clearing the way for Reeve to sail over him, hit the rail fence with his head and then land on his forehead. When he flew over the horse's head, Reeve tore the bridle, bit and reins from the animal, so that his hands were entangled in all that equipment. Had his hands been free, he would have used them to break his fall—and might have suffered nothing more serious than sprained wrists. But with his hands tangled, he fell on his head. As horrified onlookers rushed to help him, Reeve lay crumpled, very still and not breathing.

A bystander who was a doctor gave Reeve mouth-to-mouth resuscitation until an emergency medical crew arrived to resuscitate him. Reeve was taken by ambulance to the local Culpeper hospital. Although the hospital was not equipped to handle such an emergency, it did have a drug called methylprednisolone, which reduces inflammation in spinal cord injuries if given within eight hours of the injury. As soon as he was considered stable—less than one hour after the accident—Reeve was flown by helicopter to the University of Virginia Medical Center in Charlottesville.

Dana Reeve was in their motel room in Culpeper, with Will taking a nap, when she got the call. At the emergency room, she was told to wait in the lounge and a doctor would be right out. No one told her anything of her husband's condition, but when she saw a helicopter land in the hospital courtyard, she thought, "That's not for a broken arm." Finally the doctor called her to his office, told her that Reeve had broken his two top cervical vertebrae (C1 and C2) and was on a respirator. He didn't use the words "broken neck," but he advised her to say goodbye to her husband before he was airlifted to the University of Virginia research hospital. Reeve later wrote in his 1998 autobiography that Dana felt like she was being punched repeatedly and had to prepare herself each time for the next blow. People around her were talking about funeral arrangements. And all the time she was trying to keep Will amused and prevent him from being scared. To this day, Reeve regrets that their two-year-old son heard all that.

Dana Reeve, a doctor's daughter, called her

father, who said, "Oh, God," and she knew then how serious the accident had been. She went back to the motel, packed their belongings, and took time to kick a few balls with Will, who did not understand what had happened and wanted to play soccer. It was easier for her to kick the ball with him than to tell him about his father's condition. Then mother and son drove to the University of Virginia.

At a press conference in Charlottesville, doctors announced that although the helmet Reeve wore protected the actor from brain damage, he had fractured the first and second cervical vertebrae of his spinal column. These are the vertebrae in the neck, closest to the skull—and Reeve was totally paralyzed, unable even to breathe on his own. The doctors said that Reeve had apparently not suffered brain damage but they refused to predict whether or not the paralysis would be permanent. Reeve was forty-two years old, a man in the prime of life, and with a promising career ahead of him. Ironically, the man who had soared as Superman was very much earth-bound.

Reeve's family gathered at the hospital, including his wife Dana, and their son, Will; Gae Exton, the Englishwoman who is the mother of Reeve's two older children—Matthew, then sixteen, and Alexandra, then twelve; his long-divorced parents—his mother, Barbara Johnson, a reporter from Princeton, New Jersey, and his father, Franklin, a novelist and professor of creative writing at Connecticut's Wesleyan University; his brother, Benjamin, a lawyer; and numerous half- and step-siblings.

Reeve's mother wanted the doctors to pull the plug on her son. Reeve later told Barbara Walters of the television show "20/20" that his mother was responding to his oft-repeated statement that if he couldn't ride and sail and dive and do all the things he enjoyed, he wouldn't want to live. Barbara Johnson became upset, trying to convince doctors and chaplains.

Dana Reeve insisted that any decision must be made by Reeve himself. She would later insist that doctors discuss everything with Reeve personally and that nothing be done without his consent. For several days she sat beside her unconscious husband. Although he drifted into consciousness occasionally, he had no idea of his condition. When he did regain consciousness four days later, Reeve's head had been placed in a metal ring to hold it still, and he was on antibiotics for pneumonia. He has often said that he thought, "This can't be my life. There's a mistake."

He developed ICU psychosis—a mental condition resulting from the disruption of sleep patterns—in the ICU. As he suffered hallucinations and made strange comments to Dana, she feared a brain injury. But doctors reassured her that there was no brain damage.

Dana, Reeve writes in *Still Me,* was the one who held everything together during those dramatic days. She dealt with the media, kept in touch with Reeve's agent and publicist, contacted friends and relatives, and all the while kept young Will from realizing the calamity that swirled around him.

THE WILL TO LIVE

Doctors recommended surgery. According to neurosurgeon Dr. John A. Jane, Reeve's primary physician, there was no precedent for the operation, and they would have to improvise as they went along. When doctors explained the surgery to Reeve, he simply told them to do whatever they had to do. He was still convinced this was a temporary problem.

However, after the doctors carefully explained to Reeve the severity of the damage to his spinal cord, he began to realize how different this injury was from others he'd suffered and survived. If his injury had been at C5-C6 (cervical vertebrae 5 and 6), Reeve would have been able to use his arms and breathe on his own. But a C1-C2 injury is as bad as it gets. His injury was called a "hangman's injury" in horse-riding jargon because it is

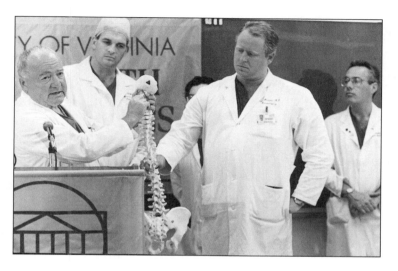

*Dr. John A. Jane explains Reeve's
condition at a press conference.*

the same cervical break that occurs in people who
are hanged. In effect, his head was disconnected
from his body.

Reeve later admitted to a biographer that
once he understood the gravity of his situation
and the risks of the surgery, he wasn't sure it was
worth it. He wasn't sure he had the will to live.
When Dana came to his bedside, he mouthed the
words to her, "Maybe we should let me go." His
wife told him that was his decision, and she would
support whatever he decided. But she told him,
"You're still you. And I love you." Reeve told television host Oprah Winfrey that if Dana had hesi-

tated or looked away, he might have had some doubt, but her reaction was instantaneous and direct. Dana later told Ann Curry of the "Today" show that she didn't feel she could ask him to stay around just because she wanted him, but that what she said came spontaneously and from the heart. Her words inspired the title of his autobiography, *Still Me*.

Reeve was also given determination by the presence of his three children who made him realize that he had to fight to live for them. When they came into his hospital room, he has said, he could see that they wanted and needed him to stay around. At first, Will was terrified of the ICU. It took him several days to overcome his fear but Dana convinced him that his father was still the same, just lying down. Soon he was breezing in and out of the ICU and making himself completely at home.

Comedian-actor Robin Williams, who had been Reeve's roommate at the Juilliard School in New York City, encouraged Reeve in the early days after his accident. Reeve recalls hearing a Russian accent and looking up from his hospital bed to see Williams in brightly colored scrub clothes. Williams proceeded to do a routine of comic one-liners, complimenting Reeve on his new tie (his respirator tube).

And Reeve was besieged with letters and

calls, telegrams from heads of state, and a letter from President Bill Clinton, who had tried to call but was unable to get through. Reeve claims Clinton finally had to give up and get back to running the country.

Reeve underwent a 6½–hour operation on June 5. The surgical team had done several practice runs to test the new technique. Dr. Jane tied the first and second vertebrae together, using a bone graft from Reeve's hip as a wedge between them. With titanium wire, he connected the first vertebra to Reeve's skull, essentially reattaching Reeve's head to his body. According to Dr. Jane, Reeve might then begin some early rehabilitation, but no one thought he would breathe on his own or recover much feeling or movement.

Some doctors believe that the state a patient is in immediately after surgery is what will be permanent; others believe recovery can come six months, a year, even five years later. Jane told Reeve he believed there was a good chance he would eventually be off the ventilator and he could expect significant return of sensation and function. He was a constant bearer of good tidings, although Reeve began to suspect that the doctor wanted to make him feel better—and wanted to make himself feel better about his patient.

Reeve's moods ranged from gratitude to horror, self-pity, confusion, and anger, in the days following the surgery. He would flare in anger at a woman doctor who treated him as though he were a child, or at his stepmother who tried to encourage Reeve by reminding him about all the things he could still do. The days were tolerable; the nights were difficult with sleepless time measured only by being turned in bed so that his skin wouldn't tear or by having someone drain the fluid from his lungs. Reeve was afraid to take his eyes off the monitors that kept track of his vital statistics, thinking something would go wrong and no one would come in time to fix it.

Reeve prayed, he says in *Still Me*, but he felt like a phony until his friend Robert Kennedy, Jr., told him, "Just fake it till you make it. The prayers will seem phony, but one day they'll become real, and your faith will become real." Reeve believes that spirituality—a belief in some higher power—helped him reach a new way of thinking about himself.

After the operation, Reeve had no appetite. A favorite aunt arranged for a local restaurant to prepare whatever Reeve wanted to eat—and then fed him. Having to be fed, he admits, was one of the most difficult adjustments he had to make.

Three weeks after surgery, he had to choose a rehabilitation institute. He finally chose the Kessler Institute for Rehabilitation in West

Orange, New Jersey, not only because of its outstanding reputation but because all his family lived relatively nearby. With the support of his family and friends, Reeve remained hopeful about his recovery.

He visualized himself getting well. Someone had sent him a picture of the Pyramid of Quetzalcoatl, the Mayan temple in Mexico. He had the postcard taped to the bottom of the monitor, so that he could always see it, and he began to imagine himself climbing those steps, one at a time, until he finally reached the top and flew into the sky.

Reeve dreams of climbing the steps at the Temple of Quetzalcoatl in Mexico.

CHAPTER TWO

REEVE AS A YOUNG ACTOR

Christopher Reeve was born on September 25, 1952, in New York City, where his father—the novelist, poet, and Russian literature scholar known as F. D. Reeve—was working on a master's degree at Columbia University. Like most student families, they had little money. His father Franklin worked at a variety of jobs to support his new family, including appearing in theater productions with political themes—which may have inspired Christopher's own involvement with both theater and politics.

The Reeve family boasted impressive ancestors, including French nobles who held titles and one who was an ambassador for Louis XIV. The first ancestor to come to America, William d'Olier, founded cotton mills in Philadelphia in the mid-1800s and established the family's wealth. Christopher's great-grandfather, Franklin d'Olier, was one of the founders of the American Legion, an organization of veterans who were devoted to patriotic causes. Among the other founders was Theodore Roosevelt, president of the United States from 1901 to 1909.

Christopher's father had graduated from Princeton University in 1950 with a degree in English and, in November 1951, married Barbara Pitney Lamb. Barbara had a very different family background than her husband. Barbara's father was a self-made man born into a working-class family in Ohio, who had become a senior partner in one of New York's most prestigious law firms. Barbara Reeve was twenty when Christopher was born. A year later, Christopher's brother, Benjamin, was born. Benjamin is now a writer and lawyer.

Reeve's parents divorced in 1956, and Barbara took the boys to Princeton to live. It was a bitter divorce, with the two parents refusing to speak to each other, making life for the boys difficult.

Both parents remarried and both had new youngsters, so that Christopher eventually found himself one of eleven children with one full brother, four step-siblings, and five half-siblings. Christopher was raised in Princeton by his mother and her new husband, banker Tristam Johnson, whom he has described as both generous and strict but a man who always wanted the best for his stepsons. Johnson put Reeve through Princeton Day School, Cornell University, and the Juilliard School. He was also the kind of man who would take his stepsons to father-son workshops where they built birdhouses, or let a young boy steer the car while sitting next to him. Reeve never told him that by age twelve he was sneaking the car out when his mother and stepfather were away. Christopher had high hopes that they would all become a family—his mother and stepfather, himself and Ben, and their half-brothers Jeff and Kevin—but he says it never came together. Eventually Barbara and Tris divorced.

Young Reeve spent weekends in New Haven, where his father taught at Yale University. He and Benjamin found it difficult to go from one household to the other, and he once told biographer Roger Rosenblatt, "It was all just bits and pieces. You just [didn't] want to risk getting involved with people for fear that things were going to [fall] apart."

His weekends in New Haven with his father added an intellectual background to his childhood, although his mother took him regularly to performances of the Princeton Society for Musical Amateurs where he sat in the soprano section with her. In 1962, the elder Reeve published *Robert Frost in Russia,* a book that resulted from his trip two years earlier to Russia to serve as Frost's translator. F. D. Reeve translated five novels by the famed Russian writer Ivan Turgenev and also wrote several novels of his own.

Christopher found his father hard to understand—full of fun and interest in his sons' lives at one moment, and remote and distant the next. Christopher spent much of his time hungering for praise and doing whatever he could to be perfect. When he was nine, his father asked him to row alone across the lake in the Poconos to a small store for pipe tobacco—it was, he recalls, a moment in the sun. And when, at twelve, he wrote a short story, his father was full of praise. But these moments were balanced by times when his father seemed to care less and less about what happened to the boy. In the late 1980s, his relationship with his father broke down almost completely, only to be restored after Reeve's accident when there was a new reaching out on both sides.

Reeve also found the difference in households difficult. His father's house was full of books, and there were important visitors and long hours of stimulating conversation. In his father's company, Christopher met poets Robert Frost and Robert Penn Warren and sociologist (later Senator) Daniel Patrick Moynihan. By contrast, his mother's house began to seem dull to him, though he writes in *Still Me* that he has gained a real respect for his mother. Always interested in writing, she eventually became associate editor of a local newspaper in Princeton, bought her own house, and took up rowing at the age of sixty. Today, she is a serious competitor.

Reeve's interest in athletics surfaced early. By six, he was skiing in the Pocono Mountains of Pennsylvania and he soon played a mean game of tennis. At school he played varsity hockey and took fencing lessons. His father taught him to sail, and he eventually raced his father's sailboat, winning most races by being demanding of his crew. He was, by his own admission, competitive. "If someone says, 'You've got to try twenty repetitions of this exercise,'" he told an interviewer, "that gives me an incentive to do thirty or thirty-five. You have to push."

HIS FIRST STAGE ROLE

Christopher's first stage role came at Princeton's McCarter Theatre when he was nine years old. After auditioning by singing, "mi, mi, mi," he was given a soprano role in Gilbert and Sullivan's *The Yeoman of the Guard.* Neither he nor his family knew it at the time, but his career goal was decided by that one small role. He began to appear in almost every theatrical performance presented at his day school and played child roles at the McCarter in such plays as *The Diary of Anne Frank* and Thornton Wilder's *Our Town.* Biogra-

Reeve at the McCarter Theatre in Princeton in 1997, where he first performed when he was nine.

pher Margaret Finn reports that he later said the theater made him feel safe, instead of "like a chess piece caught between his parents." Reeve's parents both encouraged his theatrical interest, though they never thought it would lead to a career.

A chess piece caught between his parents.

Having grown to be 6 feet 2 inches (188 cm) by the time he was fourteen, Reeve was taller than most of his classmates and felt awkward. Although he was already strikingly good-looking, he was self-conscious. But in the theater he lost his self-consciousness.

The summer of 1968 marked the beginnings of independence for the young actor. Between the ninth and tenth grades, he studied theater at the Lawrenceville School (near Princeton), and the next year he was an apprentice at the Williamstown Summer Theatre Festival in Massachusetts. He had no time to visit either of his families during the summer. At Williamstown, he got his first full taste of theater—running the sound, hanging lights, painting scenery, attending classes in voice, movement, and acting, and being part of eight plays with only fifteen Equity actors. The small size of the cast gave Reeve a lot of opportunity to be on stage. When he was sixteen, he played in Turgenev's *A Month in the Country, Death of a Salesman, The Hostage* and *The Three-penny Opera*—all at the Loeb Drama Center in Cambridge, Massachusetts. He joined the Actors Guild and found an agent to help him get more parts.

Reeve entered Cornell University in Ithaca, New York, in 1970. He chose Cornell partly for its excellent liberal arts program and theater department, but more because it was a five-hour drive to New York City and tended to be snowed in during the winter. He thought this would prevent him from being tempted to drop out of school and go to New York. At Cornell, he learned the difference between the "acting" approach and the academic approach to acting. Reeve believes that an actor should approach a role on an emotional level and follow his instincts, rather than dealing with literary themes. He describes it as the difference between drama as literature and drama as a living presence.

Throughout his college career, in spite of the snow-closed highways, Reeve traveled to New York to try out for films and television and continued to perform at regional summer theaters. The summer before his senior year, he was offered a full-time summer contract with the San Diego Shakespeare Festival at the Old Globe Theatre. After that, reluctant to return to Cornell, he took a three-month leave and headed for England and a theater tour.

When Reeve returned to Cornell in January 1973, he wanted to concentrate on acting and found it hard to settle down to the usual academic routine. With the help of the man who had hired him for the San Diego season, Reeve applied to the exclusive Drama Division at the Juilliard School in New York. The audition was nerve-wracking, but Reeve took control by rearranging the furniture on the set. He performed a monologue and then a contrastingly light and humorous piece. Three weeks later, a letter informed him that he had been accepted into the Advanced Program beginning on September 15. He could study at Juilliard and still complete his degree from Cornell. At Juilliard he studied voice, ballet, fencing, stage fighting, acrobatics, circus, mime—anything that would make him a well-rounded actor. After graduation from Cornell, he stayed at Juilliard another year. But he had to find a job to pay for his schooling when his stepfather had difficulty paying his tuition.

EARNING A LIVING

At Juilliard, Reeve became friends with Robin Williams, the zany comedic actor who later starred in the television series "Mork and Mindy" and the movies *Mrs. Doubtfire, The Birdcage, Good Morning, Vietnam,* and many others. The two were complete opposites—Reeve taking everything seriously and Williams seeing quirky humor in almost every situation—which may well have been the foundation of their friendship.

Most young, aspiring actors go from one small role to another, living hand-to-mouth. Reeve almost immediately found work that paid well—playing a tennis bum on the soap opera "Love of

Christopher Reeve as Ben Harper on Love of Life

Life." Undoubtedly his good looks were one of the reasons he landed the job. He had grown from being an awkward, too-tall adolescent into a handsome, self-assured man with strong features, thick dark hair, and sparkling blue eyes. However, he soon found that the job was taking too much time from his schooling, says biographer Margaret

Finn, and he listened to the advice of actor and director John Houseman. "Mr. Reeve," said Houseman, "it is terribly important that you become a serious classical actor. Unless of course, they offer you a [load] of money to do something else." Reeve left school and threw himself into *Love of Life,* even though he didn't like the sentimental nature of the material. "In college," he told biographer Adrian Havill, "you perform masterpieces, the classics. It isn't like that in real life."

Reeve continued to perform in repertory theater in New York with small companies that regularly performed several works in sequence. His big break came in 1975 when he was cast as Katharine Hepburn's grandson in *A Matter of Gravity.* To work opposite the great Hepburn was one of the best acting lessons he could have had. He told interviewer Jack Kroll that the renowned actress said to him, "Be fascinating, Christopher, be fascinating." He remembers thinking, "That's easy for you to do. The rest of us have to work at it." She taught him the importance of bringing his own personality to a role rather than disappearing into the character he played. But he found Hepburn a lot like his father: "Two perfectionists: loving, charismatic, charming, and able to undercut you in a second."

During the winter of 1975–76, Reeve toured with the play in Philadelphia, Washington, New

Haven, Boston, and Toronto and still maintained his work schedule on *Love of Life*. He lived on candy bars and coffee and thought he could handle it because he was young. One night, on the stage in *A Matter of Gravity,* he collapsed just after his opening line. Hepburn turned to the audience and said, "This boy's a goddamn fool. He doesn't eat enough red meat." The curtain came down, and the understudy completed the performance.

In spite of Hepburn's presence, the play was not a critical success. Reeve was praised by one critic for "having done justice to a role that required only his presence." He felt a sense of disappointment that the play didn't come alive and he did not believe, as many told him, that playing opposite Hepburn was reward enough. Just as he'd been competitive in sports, he wanted to be nothing but the best in theater.

Reeve dropped out of *A Matter of Gravity* when it moved to Los Angeles in April 1976. Then Reeve went to Hollywood, where he landed his first role in a movie made for large-screen theater. The movie, *Gray Lady Down*, was about a submarine disaster. Critics called it a disaster about a disaster. Reeve went on to other small live-theater roles.

CHAPTER THREE

REEVE BECOMES SUPERMAN

In January 1977, Reeve received a surprise call. He was asked to interview for "a big movie with a major studio." The call brought dramatic changes in Reeve's life and career. He was playing at the Circle Repertory Company in *My Life* and he agreed to go to the interview but without much expectation. However, he told author David Michael Petrou, who chronicled the making of the movie, "I always take a reading for whatever it is, even if it's the lead role in *The Joy of Cooking*."

He was introduced to the father-and-son directors Ilya and Alexander Salkind, who were looking for a young actor to play the lead role in a new production of *Superman*. Ilya Salkind had seen Reeve's picture in *Academy Players Directory*, and they wanted an unknown who looked the part—square-jawed and athletic.

Reeve's schedule had been hard on his health.

On his tall frame, the 180 pounds (81 kilograms) he now weighed made him look slight. He thought he looked like anything *but* Superman. To his surprise, the script for Superman was delivered to his home the morning after the interview. He was asked to fly to London for a reading. After finishing the script, Reeve overcame his doubts about accepting the role, if it was offered. He had been afraid that playing a comic-strip character in a not-so-serious movie would damage his career rather than further it. The Superman story was so familiar to Americans that it was almost trite, but this was a new approach. He also felt he had something to offer the movie by playing Superman as a contemporary male in an age when the masculine image had changed and men could show gentleness and vulnerability. He tried to downplay the hero aspect and to create more of a contrast between Superman and Clark Kent. Reeve records in *Still Me* that on the way back to the airport, after the London reading, his driver said, "I'm not supposed to tell you this, but you got the part."

A subsequent screen test was a success. Reeve was a perfect Clark Kent, and as Superman, wearing a padded suit to fill out his thin frame, "he virtually exploded onto the screen," Salkind said. Reeve's phone rang late in February. His agent told him Rona Barrett had announced on *Good Morning, America* that Reeve had the part. Salkind called soon after to confirm. The signing salary was $250,000. Reeve was later further reassured to learn that some serious and respected actors had signed on for the project—Gene Hackman and Marlon Brando among them.

Superman first appeared as a comic-book character in the late 1930s. In 1940 the superhero appeared on radio. Three movies followed—*Superman* (1948), *Atom Man vs. Superman* (1950), and *Superman and the Mole Men* (1951). By 1951, the superhero was also on what was then the new small screen—television. George Reeves, who had played Superman in *Superman and the Mole Men,* starred in the series. The series ended in 1957, but the original 104 episodes were shown on television for years. After the series and the movies, Americans might well have been expected to yawn at the idea of yet another reincarnation of the Clark Kent/Superman story.

The Salkinds' script had a history of its own. Mario Puzo, author of *The Godfather,* wrote the first version, but it was dark and tragic. The Salkinds hired lesser-known writers to shorten the script and make it lighter in tone. They didn't want to lose the spirit of the comic book, but wanted the movie to rise above the comic strip. They incorporated the love triangle—Clark Kent loves Lois Lane and she loves Superman.

George Reeves as Superman in
Superman and the Mole Men

The final version of the script was true to the original Superman story: When the planet Krypton blows up, Superman's parents—Jor-El (Marlon Brando) and Lara (Susannah York) send their young child to Earth where he is raised by Kansas farmers Jonathan and Martha Clark. When his true identity is revealed to him, Superman spends the next twelve years living at the North Pole. Then, at the age of thirty, he becomes Clark Kent, reporter on *The Daily Planet,* a newspaper in the town of Metropolis. He falls in love with Lois Lane, also a reporter on the *Planet.* As Superman he fights crime, saves Lane's life, and, by stopping the earth's rotation, prevents a massive earthquake from destroying the West Coast.

The Salkind story is divided into three parts. The movie opens in the science-fiction world of Krypton, with chrome, glass, and white lights and then it moves to the wheat fields and blue skies of Kansas. The final portion of the movie is set in the city of Metropolis, where Superman (or Clark Kent) is quickly involved with archvillain Lex Luthor (Gene Hackman) and his girlfriend Miss Tessmacher (Valerie Perrine), his editor-in-chief Perry White (Jackie Cooper), and, of course, Lane.

HOW DOES SUPERMAN FLY?

Reeve went to London, where his first job was to gain weight. He ate four meals a day, drank protein milkshakes, took vitamins, and worked out daily. Eventually he went from 180 to 220 pounds (81 to 100 kg), and his body became muscular enough to be believable as Superman.

True to his spirit, Reeve did his own stunts. To take off in flight and land again, he used a trampoline. Other shots required harnesses, which eventually caused bruises and calluses, and cranes, which required him to keep his arms and legs perfectly straight while supposedly soaring through the air. What helped him most was his own joy in flying, whether

"You must see on a man's face a certain delight, a certain joy in flying that can only come out of inner conviction."

Although it may have looked easy, pretending to fly through the air was hard work.

in an airplane, a seaplane, a glider, or freely as Superman. He told *Newsweek* reporter Jack Kroll, "You must see on a man's face a certain delight, a certain joy in flying that can only come out of inner conviction."

John Barry, a member of the production staff, told a story about Reeve being hoisted 200 feet (61 m) off the ground in bitter cold weather. He had better physical coordination than their usual stuntmen. "I asked him if [the height] bothered him and he said that after the first fifty feet it didn't make any difference to him, he stopped caring about it. That attitude never changed, even though a couple of times he got closer to really flying than most people would want."

On the set, Reeve gained a reputation for seriousness. He didn't party with the crew, and he didn't joke around. He went home every day as soon as shooting was over to study the day's filming and worry about how he could have done better. Reeve no doubt felt the double weight of two very different roles—in one he was the superhero who flew through the air, rescued distressed damsels, and stopped the earth's rotation; in the other, he was Clark Kent—the shy, bumbling, always awkward newspaper reporter with his boring business suits and owlish eyeglasses.

Much of the filming was done in England, but for outdoor city scenes, the crew went back to New

*Superman (Reeve) takes Lois Lane (Margot Kidder)
for a ride above the city.*

York City. One July night in New York, Reeve was
hooked into his flying rig, fastened to the crane,
and then hoisted into the air. Suddenly traffic
stopped below him, and crowds began to applaud,
calling out "It's Superman!"

One popular scene from the movie has Superman taking Lois Lane on a dream-flight high
above the towers and bridges of New York City. He
deposits her gently on the terrace of her apartment and soars off into the night sky. As Lois

Lane, overcome with her love for Superman, stumbles into her living room, the doorbell rings. There stands Clark Kent, reminding her of their date for the evening.

When the shooting of the movie ran behind schedule, Warner Brothers threatened to cut off funding. Scheduled to be through production and ready for editing in October, the movie was almost five months late. In April, Reeve filmed final scenes in which he appeared to be shooting through the earth's red-hot molten layer to change its rotation briefly and prevent an earthquake. In August, the London Symphony Orchestra recorded the score, and Reeve had only a few more shots to film, this time in New Mexico.

The end of shooting for a film is traditionally celebrated with a "wrap" party—for "wrapping up" the project. At the end of *Superman*, instead of attending the wrap party, Reeve skippered a sailboat from Connecticut to Bermuda.

Finally, after three years of planning and two years of filming in three studios, and in eight countries on three continents, with a thousand people working on the production and a record-breaking $40-million cost, *Superman* was ready for its world premiere. The film was released to 700 movie theaters in the United States on December 15, 1978, and by the end of the first week it had grossed $12 million. This may not sound like a lot by today's standards, but then it was the largest one-week gross in Warner Brothers' history. The opening had been preceded by a worldwide promotion campaign that included planes, helicopters, blimps, and sailboats announcing the coming film. Crowds flocked to the movie theaters, and Reeve drew high praise from the critics. "Ridiculously good-looking" wrote one, while another claimed "The easy authority with which Reeve handles the double role is the real surprise of the picture."

Years later, Reeve told reporter Michael Bandler that there was "an uncanny meeting of actor and role in *Superman.* It was my kind of naiveté, my sense of optimism, a basic belief in people, my athletic background and love of flying all combined. And I'm glad that it's given the mothers of America an alternative to *Rambo* for their kids."

While filming *Superman,* Reeve met British model Gae Exton. By the time the film was showing in American theaters, the two were sharing an apartment in New York, and when fans wrote to ask if he was married, they were told that he was seriously involved with a woman. The phone in that apartment rang constantly, and the mailbox bulged with scripts: Christopher Reeve had become an overnight star. But fame did not go to his head nor make him less serious about his career. To his agent's dismay, he rejected the lead

Reeve with Gae Exton

role (and $1 million) in *American Gigolo* because he disliked the script. Instead, Richard Gere shot to fame in the role. Reeve chose a role in a low-budget film that he described as an old-fashioned romance, rather than a story based on bedroom scenes. The movie, *Somewhere in Time,* was a gentle time-travel love story filmed in period costume on Mackinac Island in Lake Michigan—a tranquil, nineteenth-century community which to this day allows no automobiles. The film, while neither commercially nor critically successful, increased Reeve's reputation as an "actor's actor," one who took his work seriously.

By now, he was the subject of countless magazine articles. But they were never about his aspirations as a serious actor; they were either about Superman or about his relationship with Gae Exton. Reeve would not talk about Exton or his private life. Michael Bandler, writing for *McCall's,* said, "He'll tell you, politely but firmly—and not in so many words—that it's none of your business."

CHAPTER FOUR

MORE ADVENTURES AS SUPERMAN

Reeve was under contract for two Superman movies. For the second one, the Salkinds doubled his salary. He once again had doubts, but Reeve found that he liked the script, although it was heavier with evil than the first movie. In *Superman II*, the hero hurls a terrorist's bomb into space, where it shatters the prison—also floating in space—of three exiled Kryptonite criminals. They take over Earth while Superman is in his North Pole hideaway—the Fortress of Solitude—with Lois Lane. The not-so-subtle message is that Superman is not paying attention to business. He has in fact lost his power because he has fallen in love and let love distract him. When he learns of the takeover, he mysteriously regains his capabilities, outsmarts the three criminals and their henchman Lex Luthor (the villain of the first movie) and saves Earth. Reeve thinks it may be

Reeve as Superman at the North Pole in Superman II

the best of the series because it has moments of good comedy.

Superman II was released in Britain in December 1980, but not in the United States until June 1981. It, too, earned rave reviews as a powerful sequel and a smash success. *The New Yorker* magazine's influential film critic Pauline Kael wrote, "Christopher Reeve['s] . . . transitions from Clark Kent to Superman and back are now polished comedy routines." She praised the exact effect—the contrast between the two roles—that Reeve wanted to achieve.

Reeve had now played in two of the highest grossing movies of all time. He was given the British Academy of Motion Picture Arts and Sciences Award as the Best Actor of 1979 for his role in the first movie. But in his own country, the Academy of Motion Picture Arts and Sciences neither nominated him for an Oscar nor invited him into membership. Some saw it as an insult to both Reeve and the movie. He was, however, named one of the Ten Outstanding Americans by the United States Jaycees.

LIFE CHANGES FOR "SUPERMAN"

Reeve had other things on his mind. In December 1979, Gae Exton gave birth to their son, Matthew. The proud father was irritated when the tabloids referred to the infant as "Superbaby," but he was learning that his sudden rise to fame brought with it such hindrances as overwhelming media attention.

Other stories illustrate the way fame had changed Reeve's life. Reporter Fred Yager tells of

Reeve and Exton with their son Matthew in 1975

being in Reeve's New York apartment when some schoolchildren called through the intercom: "Can Superman come out and play?" Reeve's reply was, "Not today. He's got somebody to save." Another time, he and a friend left their bikes outside a bar. In a split second, the bikes were stolen. Reeve ran down the street, saw a man riding his bike, chased and caught him. He threw the man on the sidewalk and was lifting him up by the lapels, when the would-be thief screamed, "Oh, no, Superman! I'm sorry!" Reeve let the man go and took his bike.

Once again, Reeve disappointed his agent by turning down a $1-million movie role. Instead, he returned to Williamstown to play live theater—for $225 a week—and then to the Broadway production of *Fifth of July,* a play about a Vietnam vet who is a double amputee, a role which contrasted dramatically with the heroic stature of Superman. The play called for him to openly express his depression over his disability. Reeve could not know how this foreshadowed his own future.

Reeve left the play in April 1981 to star in the movie *Deathtrap*, and then spent the summer back at Williamstown. Next he starred in *Sleeping Beauty* for a cable television production. After that came the movie, *Monsignor,* for which Reeve assumed a totally new character, unlike any of his previous roles. He played a corrupt priest who betrayed a young nun and schemed to win the favor of the Vatican by getting money for the Holy City any way he could. Though Catholics hated the movie and critics didn't like it much either, Reeve had now proved that he could play a variety of roles and didn't always have to be Superman.

The third Superman movie was being written, and Reeve knew he would star in it only if he liked the script. He did like it, and by now his price had gone from $250,000 for the first movie, and $500,000 for the second, to $2 million for *Superman III*.

Reeve during the making of Deathtrap *in 1982*

SUPERMAN III

In *Superman III*, the character of the superhero takes a new direction once again. The villain, Ross Webster, creates a synthetic piece of kryptonite and persuades Superman to accept it as an award. Superman fans know that kryptonite is the one substance that can render their hero powerless, or even kill him; in this instance, it does neither. Instead, it creates an evil Superman who does such things as blow out the eternal Olympic flame, cause an oil spill, abandon accident victims, and is generally the exact opposite of his usual self. Playing the evil Superman allowed Reeve to add a third dimension to the role—and thus gave him another chance to display his acting versatility. That acting ability was the only thing that saved the movie. Critics generally thought it lacked the power and scope of the first two films.

Superman III was released in June 1983. Reeve was now a star—one of Hollywood's "hunks" according to an issue of *Newsweek* that featured him on the cover—and roles were offered right and left. He turned down another $1-million movie role to play a defeated Southern gentleman after the Civil War in a movie version of novelist Henry James' 1886 book, *The Bostonian*. He followed this with a movie called *The Aviator*, filmed in Yugoslavia. It drew such poor critical response that it was released to only a few theaters. Reeve went on to another Henry James novel, this time *The Aspern Papers,* in a live production opposite famed British actress Vanessa Redgrave. Eventually, the two Henry James pieces brought him critical praise as a serious actor—which had always been his goal. His decision to turn down lucrative jobs in favor of meaningful roles brought him the artistic satisfaction he sought, even if it did upset his agent.

Reeve and Exton were apart more than they were together in these times—he was working in various locations and she remained in London, where she now ran a modeling agency. But when she gave birth to daughter Alexandra, Reeve flew to London to be with her.

Reeve was disappointed when he lost two big movie roles, in *Children of a Lesser God* (to William Hurt) and in *The Running Man* (to Arnold Schwartzenegger). He was beginning to realize what his agent had told him all along: the artistically satisfying roles on TV or in live theater did not bring in the money that major feature films did. By now, he needed that income to support what had become a lavish lifestyle, with houses in England, California, Massachusetts, and New York City, three airplanes and a yacht. He went back to television for a production of the classic Russian novel *Anna Karenina,* and for documentaries such as one about Dutch artist Vincent Van Gogh, another about dinosaurs, and even a drivers' safety special. But now, whatever he did, critics linked him to the Superman role in their reviews. He swore he would never again play Superman.

SUPERMAN IV

While Reeve had pledged not to take on the role of Superman again, he changed his mind when he was offered the part at a time that he needed the money. Two Israeli cousins had purchased the rights to the Superman films from the Salkinds, and they offered him $3 million for the movie in addition to $1 million for another movie of his choice. He chose *Street Smart*, a story about a reporter who makes up a story in order to win fame and a good job on television. But the reporter becomes caught in his own trap when a district attorney thinks his fictional character is a real suspect on trial. Reeve described his character in *Street Smart* as a "weasel." It was another villainous role like the one he played in *Monsignor*. Fans did not like the movie. Most moviegoers saw him flying through the air no matter what role he played, and they had a hard time reconciling Superman with a weasel.

Reeve was like his movie character in *Street*

Trying to break away from his Superman image, Reeve played an ambitious reporter who lies to achieve fame in Street Smart.

Smart—caught in his own trap. He had signed a contract to play yet another Superman role because he needed the money, but he didn't want to play the part. *Superman IV: The Quest for Peace* was filmed in England, with many actors from the first movie, including Gene Hackman, Margot Kidder, Jackie Cooper, and Susannah York. This one involves a new love triangle—the daughter of the *Daily Planet*'s new owner falls in love with Clark Kent, while Lois Lane discovers

Reeve takes flight again as Superman in
Superman IV: The Quest for Peace.

she is still in love with Superman. At the movie's
end, Superman hurls all the world's nuclear
weapons into the sun and lectures the United
Nations on peace.

Critics called the movie incomplete, praising
its early scenes and then complaining that it just

seemed to fade away into a dramatic ending for which the audience was unprepared. Actually, the movie *was* unfinished. The producers ran out of money and simply released the film where they stopped shooting.

For Reeve, it was an artistic embarrassment. In *Still Me,* he writes, "The less said about *Superman IV* the better." Yet he completed the filming because he was under contract and because the jobs of many others, including the production crew, depended on his

> **"The less said about *Superman IV* the better."**

being there. The few bright notes, for Reeve, were that both of his children appeared in a scene in that movie, and he took Matthew aloft in the flying rig. It was, *McCall's* quoted him as saying, no more important to the boy than "the sharing we get by riding bikes in the park. It's really a shared activity between father and son, not 'My dad's Superman.'"

Reeve probably would not have done a fifth Superman film under any circumstances. He told *People* magazine in an interview for its June 12, 1995 issue that "I'm in pretty good shape, but my guess is that people don't want to see Superman with a spare tire hanging over his yellow belt." The same article quotes the actor as having said,

"Older faces are more interesting—particularly my face, which was a little on the bland side when I was younger." It's an interesting thought coming from a man who was described, in his youth, as "ridiculously good-looking."

In *Still Me,* Reeve writes that he was the right actor for the part at the time, but he thinks the role needs to be reinterpreted from generation to generation.

CHAPTER FIVE

LIFE AFTER SUPERMAN

Reeve went back to the United States after the filming, and this time he left Gae Exton and his two children behind in England. He and Exton agreed they had grown apart both physically and emotionally.

That summer—even before the August 1987 premiere of *Superman IV*—Reeve met Dana Morosini, a young actress who was singing in a cabaret near the Williamstown Theatre where he was then playing. He had been alone for five months and was determined to have a quiet and reflective summer. He was not, he said, looking for a relationship. But, he writes in *Still Me,* when Dana sang "The Music That Makes Me Dance," he went down "hook, line and sinker." When Reeve asked to meet her after her act finished one evening, he felt as awkward as a teenager. "Playing Clark Kent was no stretch for me," he wrote.

He offered her a ride to a party, but she said no, thank you, she'd take her own car. At the party, he

"Playing Clark Kent was no stretch for me."

tried again, starting a conversation. Neither now remembers what they talked about, but they stood in the middle of the floor for an hour without moving. Then, not wanting to rush things, he said, "Nice to meet you," and got in his truck and went home. The two soon settled into a courtship that included sailing—something fairly new to Dana—cross-country skiing, raising livestock, and even fishing in a pond on Reeve's farm. Once he picked her a bunch of wildflowers, then grew shy about giving them to her and asked a girl passing by the theater to deliver them for him. By the time Dana came out to thank him, he was gone, feeling he'd done something stupid.

A DARING TRIP

That November, Reeve did something not all actors would have done. He went to Chile to beg for the lives of seventy-nine playwrights, actors, and directors who had been condemned to death by Trizano, one of the death squads operated by dictator Augusto Pinochet who then controlled

Chile. The artists were accused of presenting Marxist beliefs in their works—beliefs that the government oppressed the poor and should be overthrown. A major rally was planned to try to save their lives, and organizers thought that having the star internationally known as Superman would further their cause. Ariel Dorfman, a writer and native of Chile then in exile, asked Reeve to make the trip and did not hide the fact that Reeve's life would be in danger. Christopher Reeve debated for less than an hour and then

Reeve with Dana Morosini

agreed to go to Santiago, Chile's largest city. He arrived within twenty-four hours of the scheduled executions.

On his way into the city, Reeve saw a cartoon on a billboard that showed Superman speeding through the air, the dictator in his arms. Presumably he was going to hurl Pinochet into space as he had done with the nuclear weapons. There was great fear for Reeve's safety, and he was surrounded by six bodyguards.

The rally was held in a stadium, and thousands of people chanted, "Superman, Superman—take Pinochet away." Permission had been granted for the rally, but just before it began, police used fire hoses to force the crowd away from the gates. Protestors then squeezed into an old airplane hangar. Reeve knew he might be killed if he entered that dilapidated building, but he went inside anyway. When the crowd finally stopped chanting, "Superman, Superman," Reeve began to speak. The lights went out, probably disconnected by the police who tried to disperse the crowd outside the building—but light was soon restored. Reeve read a letter from his fellow actors and told the crowd that he would tell America of their bravery. The next day Pinochet's death squad retracted the execution order. Within a year, Pinochet lost power and with him went the death squads. Many people in Chile gave part of the credit to Reeve, and the Walter Briehl Human Rights Foundation gave him two awards for bravery in 1988.

Although he was now a real-life hero, Reeve was still pegged as Superman with no new big

Reeve in Santiago, Chile, during his trip to try to save seventy-nine Chilean actors, directors, and playwrights

films coming his way. He continued to act in small, live-theater productions, from Shakespeare (where critics talked about his looks and not his acting) to a play about the Civil War where he was praised for playing two roles—a Northerner and a Southerner—with great conviction. He was still performing often at the theater in Williamstown where he had started his career.

He also returned to television. His first role was in a two-part miniseries called *The Great Escape*. It was based on the adventures of Major John Dodge who masterminded a famous 1944 escape from a German prison camp during World War II. The story had been told in a 1963 movie, which had been one of young Reeve's favorite films. He studied hard for the part, reading books on Dodge and interviewing his daughter, who lived in England. After filming *The Great Escape,* Reeve went on a national tour with a small play called *Love Letters* and received high praise for his portrayal of a man who suffers an emotional breakdown. Critics generally praised Reeve and live theater gave him great satisfaction—but it didn't fill his wallet like the Superman films had. In 1991, Reeve played in a television movie that he would not allow his children to see. He played the role of a child molester and hoped the movie would educate the parents of young children.

During the late 1980s and early 1990s, Reeve

continued his work for a variety of charitable causes. He gathered fellow stars to help save the Williamstown movie theater from destruction. Reeve also worked hard for what he considered the most important issue—saving the global atmosphere from pollution. He fought the installation of a coal-burning power plant near his Williamstown home because he was afraid it would cause air pollution and filmed public service announcements supporting a law that would

Reeve takes his children to a benefit for the Williamstown Theatre Festival.

enable the public to sue industrial polluters. Reeve even testified before Congress on behalf of what became, in April 1990, the Clean Air Act Amendments. Reeve also narrated a documentary on oil-tanker spills, concentrating on the 1989 *Exxon Valdez* spill in Alaska. In 1993 he rolled up his sleeves to help Vice President Al Gore clean up a beach in New Jersey.

Other causes caught Reeve's attention. He went on a fund-raising tour for AIDS victims and, echoing his Chilean trip, became an artists' advocate. The Creative Coalition soon had a membership of 225 well-known stars of stage and screen. Reeve and other coalition members testified before Congress when the National Endowment for the Arts was in danger of losing its funding. Conservative legislators wanted to shut down or severely limit the agency because they believed it had funded artistic works—primarily graphic arts such as drawing, painting, and photography—that went against the basic moral principles of the United States. Reeve and others called that censorship, a violation of the Bill of Rights. "Politicians," Reeve said, "should never have the power to decide what is art."

"Politicians should never have the power to decide what is art."

During the 1992 presidential campaign, Reeve worked actively for the Democratic Clinton–Gore ticket, which he supported strongly because of its emphasis on saving the environment. When President-elect Clinton asked him to speak at the inauguration gala, however, he spoke on the status of artists rather than on the environment. He told the audience, "The life of the artist is not something to be ashamed of anymore."

Meanwhile, Reeve's life with Dana Morosini

Reeve, with actors Alec Baldwin and Eric Bogosian, in Washington, D.C., to testify against artistic censorship

continued to be a love match. Although the pair were together all the time, there was no talk of marriage for quite some time. The press and even friends were curious, but Reeve later explained that what he'd seen of marriage as a young child

Reeve at the inauguration parade for Bill Clinton

made him less likely to enter into it. As he tells it, he and Dana suddenly looked at each other one night over dinner and said, "Let's get married."

They were married on his farm in Williamstown, with his two children—Matthew, then

Christopher and Dana Reeve a few months before the birth of their son

twelve, and Alexandra, then eight—and Dana's parents—Chuck and Helen Morosini—and Reeve's parents joining some fifty other guests. Reeve was thirty-nine; his bride, thirty-one.

Dana Morosini Reeve gave birth to a son, Will, in June 1992. They sold Reeve's Manhattan penthouse in order to raise their son in Westchester County, north of New York City. The farm at Williamstown was still their summer retreat.

Reeve continued filming TV movies, including the classic sea-disaster movie based on Jack London's 1904 novel, *The Sea Wolf*. He won particular critical praise for a relatively small role in *The Remains of the Day,* a novel that is set in England as World War II approaches. Reeve played an American congressman who is daringly forthright with what he calls "gentlemen amateurs in international affairs."

By 1993, Reeve was once again reading movie scripts. When he played in a romantic comedy, *Speechless*, critics predicted that he would be rediscovered, as had happened to John Travolta. Next he starred in a science-fiction movie about mind control titled *Village of the Damned.* In an almost eerie coincidence, he played a paraplegic in a film titled *Above Suspicion.*

"I went to a rehab hospital," he told Oprah Winfrey, "to learn what it was like to be a paraplegic. But every night I got in my car and drove away, and I remember thinking 'Thank God, it's not me. I can go home at night.'"

Even with his career more active, Reeve found time to support the causes he held dear. He filmed a PBS special on gray whales off the coast of Alaska. In early 1995, he went to Tucson, Ari-

Reeve in a scene from Remains of the Day

zona, to support a teacher whose plan to present a play about cancer patients, *The Shadow Box,* was under attack from parents who objected to the graphic language. Reeve and other actors performed the play in a local auditorium, and he took

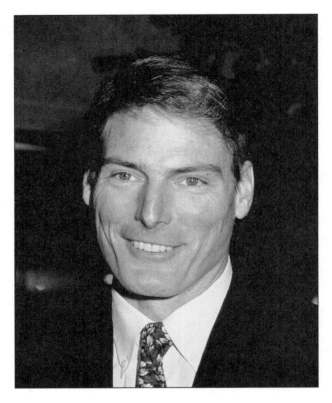

Contented and successful in 1994, Reeve never expected the challenges he would have to overcome the next year.

part in a panel discussion on censorship. That spring, The Creative Coalition again went to Washington where the National Endowment for the Arts was once more in danger. Congress finally voted to cut funding for the agency but not—as had been feared—to disband it.

Christopher Reeve was living his life to the full—an actor sought by many, an advocate for the causes he thought were important, and a happy family man. Then came that fateful day in Culpeper County, Virginia.

CHAPTER SIX

REEVE WORKS TOWARD RECOVERY

On March 25, 1996, less than a year after his accident, Christopher Reeve made a surprise appearance at the annual Academy Awards ceremony. Alone, strapped into a wheelchair but wearing a tuxedo—with the respirator tube still in place as his "tie"—he wheeled himself to the front of the stage, his wheelchair propelled by the breath he exhaled.

The crowd, having watched spectacular productions of film and music and a parade of stars, was hushed at first. Then, as one, they rose to their feet, filling the pavilion with wild applause.

At first nervous, then grinning with excitement, Reeve waited for the overwhelming applause to die down. While he waited, his eyes sparkled and he grinned widely. He was still the ever-handsome, ever-charming Christopher Reeve.

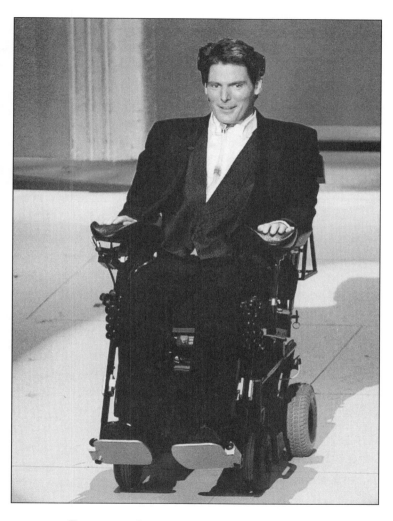

Reeve receives a warm welcome at the
Academy Awards ceremony.

"Thank you, thank you very much," he said several times. But his voice was whispery, and it didn't carry to the crowd. When the audience was finally quiet, Reeve had to wait a moment for the respirator to fill his air with lungs so that he could speak. Then he began with, "What you probably don't know is that I left New York last September, and I just arrived here this morning. And I'm glad I did, because I wouldn't have missed this kind of welcome for the world." He spoke only a few sentences at a time and then had to wait for his respirator to give him air again.

He had not wheeled himself onto the stage that night simply to be a spectacle, no matter how warm the welcome. He was there to present a segment of the show that presented highlights of films from several years that dealt with social issues. The message of the film clips—which ended with *Schindler's List*, the movie about the man who had saved so many Jews from the Nazi death camps—was that Hollywood and the film community could meet any challenge—and must. "Let us continue to take risks," he told his audience. "Let us tackle the issues in many ways. . . . there

"Let us tackle the issues in many ways. . . . there is no challenge, artistic or otherwise, that we can't meet."

is no challenge, artistic or otherwise, that we can't meet."

It had taken Christopher Reeve a lot of hard work to be able to appear before his colleagues that night . . . and a lot of hard work, and heartbreak, still lay ahead of him. And it was not his first public appearance.

He had appeared at the annual fund-raising dinner of The Creative Coalition in October 1995, when Robin Williams was to be honored. The short trip to the Pierre Hotel in New York from the Kessler Institute in West Orange, New Jersey, was as carefully orchestrated as an overseas trip by the president of the United States. Police barricades were set up to protect Reeve from paparazzi and curious crowds, and he was whisked into the hotel through the kitchen where, to his amazed pleasure, the workers stood aside and applauded. He rested in a suite, then attended a reception with a nurse all the while checking his blood pressure and the catheter bag of urine on his leg. When the guests went to dinner, he went back to his room to rest. But then it was time for him to go onstage—to a cheering ovation that lasted five minutes. For a moment, he was panicked about what to say, but then he told a funny story that revolved around his disability, and the evening went well. To the audience's delight, Williams made jokes about Reeve's wheelchair—

pretending to take the curse off it, warning that if he puffed too hard, he'd pop a wheelie and fly off into the audience. They loved it.

As he had promised his doctors, Reeve was back at Kessler by midnight. It had been a joyous experience but it had also been much more stressful than he anticipated.

THE ROAD BACK

Reeve had arrived at the Kessler Institute for Rehabilitation on June 28, 1995, barely a month after his accident. He was there for twenty-four weeks of physical therapy. He was underweight and physically frail, with a variety of medical problems, including low blood and protein counts, which had to be resolved before he could begin therapy.

Reeve recounted some of the difficulties of his early hospitalization and therapy to Oprah Winfrey on her May 4, 1998, show. Several times, both in the hospital and the rehabilitation unit, he had what is called a "pop-off"—the plastic tube of his ventilator suddenly popped off the metal pipe in his throat, depriving him of air. The ventilator is equipped with an alarm, but until someone responded to the alarm, he was helpless and unable to breathe. He described himself once as flopping around like a fish out of water. Once when he had a pop-off, the security guard in the room asked, "Are you all right, Mr. Reeve?" Reeve couldn't talk to tell him no, he wasn't all right. Reeve contends that the guard could have turned on the light and reconnected the tube himself.

After the accident, Reeve required a ventilator to breathe.

Instead, he went to look for a nurse, while Reeve thrashed around in panic and then nearly lost consciousness. Now, Reeve told Winfrey, he hasn't had a pop-off in a year, and it wouldn't be as serious since he can breathe on his own.

At Kessler, he once had an allergic reaction to a drug and could not breathe. His heart rate soared, and his blood pressure dropped dramatically. He thought he was dying and remembers thinking—and perhaps saying aloud, "I'm sorry, but I have to go now." He remembers what is often described as a near-death experience: the sensation of floating over the room and looking down at his body lying on the bed and all the people working over him. He was saved by a massive dose of epinephrine (a drug that stimulates the heart).

He also developed a bedsore, an area of infection caused by lying in one position. The bedsore was so deep that the wound went to the bone. The doctors threatened surgery. Reeve asked them to wait, and he had to lie on his side for eight days without moving.

But the most terrifying moment, he said, was when he took his first shower. He was, he confessed, more afraid of that than almost anything he had done in his action-filled life—afraid of being rolled down the hall, afraid of the water, and afraid the water would get into his tracheotomy tube and he would drown. A nurse, a Jamaican man Reeve called "Juice," convinced him to try the shower, saying "You're gonna feel so good, man. You're gonna want a shower every night." He finally tried it, but Dana had to walk into the shower and be where he could see and talk to her. Juice told him a story that made him laugh so hard that tears rolled down his face, and after that, he could take a shower.

Juice also helped him work up the courage to sit in a wheelchair, although his first time in a wheelchair also threw him into a full-blown panic attack in which he thought, "I can't do this! Get me out of here!" His chair is a "sip-and-puff" with six areas of command. To go in any direction, he sips air from a plastic straw or blows into it at various strengths. It was hard to learn to drive his chair, and Reeve hasn't yet forgotten the time he was practicing in a large open area at Kessler and crashed into a piano that a woman was playing. The piano moved about 5 feet (1.5 m), but the pianist never missed a beat. She stood up, followed the piano, and kept playing—and no one in her audience seemed to think the incident unusual.

When he first went to Kessler, he was also emotionally frail. He was not an ideal patient. He couldn't believe that he had to spend long weeks in an institution for the disabled, because he had not yet accepted himself as "one of them." Accepting your condition is an essential first step in rehabilitation, but Reeve refused to do it. He would not read a manual on spinal cord injuries until a nurse forced him to look at it. He didn't want to look at other patients, because he didn't want to believe he was like them. But gradually he began to know the patients as individuals—the young boy whose brother had flipped him on his head in a wrestling match, the stagehand who'd stepped backwards off some scaffolding, a man who was bodysurfing when a wave tossed him into the sand.

Therapy involved tasks most of us take for granted—trying to move his shoulders, trying to breathe. Sometimes for days Reeve made no progress and was ready to give up. But the therapists kept encouraging him, and every day he got a little stronger. The knowledge that he might recover months or years later motivated him.

The hardest task for Reeve was testing his vital capacity—seeing how much air he could take in on his own. For days, he could not make the meter move—he was taking in no air at all. He began to dread the test and finally said, "I can't do this, so don't make me."

But as the time neared for him to leave Kessler and return home, he realized he would have to breathe on his own. He announced he wanted to try again, and within days he was making progress that astounded the respiratory therapist. Before leaving Kessler, he breathed on his own for thirty minutes.

THE RETURN HOME

Working on a piece for *Good Housekeeping* magazine, society columnist Liz Smith asked Reeve if he experienced the expected depression when he was finally able to return to his Westchester County home. Admitting that it was an emotional experience for him, Reeve said that

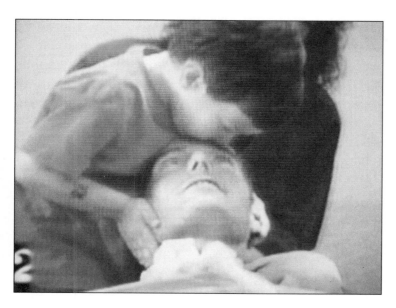

Will Reeve visits with his father.

instead of causing depression, "it was a tremendous boost. My doctor visited after a few days. He found my breathing was better. My blood pressure, oxygen levels, blood count, and protein count—everything had gone up."

Living at home has not been an easy adjustment, though for Reeve or for his family. First, they had to have the house totally remodeled to meet his medical needs. "Do you know how much an elevator costs?" he asked E!Online interviewer Ivor Davis. The answer is $70,000. An entire wing was added to the three-story house to accommodate his medical staff and equipment; doorways were widened and stairways replaced with ramps so that Reeve could wheel anywhere he wanted to go. The basement of the house provides office space for the Christopher Reeve Foundation to promote research on spinal cord injury. In addition to remodeling the house, Reeve faces health-care costs of $400,000 annually. His breath-controlled wheelchair cost $40,000.

Christopher Reeve had the financial resources to buy the expensive wheelchair and make the necessary changes in his home, though he's quick to tell you that he's not a rich man. He admits to some unwise investments in the 1980s, and he knows his health insurance will run out in about 2003. He told interviewer Ivor Davis that he figured he had five years before public interest in his situation dwindled.

Dana Reeve explains that she and Christopher are not the heroes. The true heroes are the peoples who face such a situation without resources. Asked by Barbara Walters what happens to people like him with no money, Reeve said they are put in a nursing home, and he recounted the tale of a twelve-year-old boy whose family was financially destitute. The child was put into a mental institution. It's another reason that Reeve fights so hard for research and for lifetime insurance benefits.

He has fought constantly with insurance companies. His insurance company wanted to pay for only forty-five days of home care, with a nurse on duty from seven in the morning to three in the afternoon. Outside those hours, Dana was to be responsible for his care. They refused to pay for a backup ventilator. And they saw no reason for Reeve to travel, though traveling to make speeches is now his major source of income. They also refused to pay for exercise equipment, although research emphasizes the importance of preparing the body through exercise for new treatments and therapies. Reeve has equipped his home with exercise equipment himself and appears to have won most other battles with his insurance company, but they have been hard-fought battles.

In January 1996, wealthy California horsewoman Joan Irvine Smith, impressed by Reeve's energy and commitment, donated $1 million to establish the Reeve-Irvine Center for spinal cord research at the University of California at Irvine. She also established a $50,000 annual prize for the research scientist who made the most progress in neurological research during a given year. Reeve hopes to be among the first volunteers for any scheduled experiments in nerve regeneration. He is also active in the American Paralysis Association that has only one goal—to find a cure.

Reeve with his son Matthew at press conference for new legislation on spinal injury research

Reeve is a member of the board and often speaks on behalf of the organization.

Reeve has become extremely knowledgeable about the technical aspects of spinal cord injury and recovery. He willingly tells listeners that the reason the condition has not aroused the public interest—in the way, for instance, that cancer or AIDS have—is that the condition has always been considered beyond treatment. Over the years, many victims died prematurely of pneumonia. Reeve can trace research into the condition from the 1830s to the present, and he is convinced that the current push for a cure is based on reality, not blind optimism. For a while, he admits, he was so involved in talking to research scientists and plotting strategies that he neglected his own rehabilitation.

DAILY LIVING

Reeve's day begins when he awakens at 8:00 A.M. It takes three hours to get him ready for the day, whereas most of us can dress and get ready in an hour or less. His day begins with what he calls "ranging," where aides move his arms and legs to keep them flexible. Then electric stimulation, including a pair of pants with electrodes in them, is used to stimulate his muscles and keep them from wasting away. Several times a week he is strapped to a tilt-table which brings him as close as possible to a standing position—preparation for the day when he can once again stand on his own.

After a sponge bath, two aides put his pants on him. He admitted on television that the loss of self-control and spontaneity symbolized by having to be dressed like a baby, is hard on him. Twice a day, he practices breathing on his own for half-hour sessions. If necessary, he can breathe up to two hours off the ventilator. By 11:00 A.M., he is ready for the day's work, including writing correspondence and speeches. The evening, he says, is family time, but he starts to prepare for bed at 9:30 P.M. It takes about two hours, he told Barbara Walter, "to put me away." In his autobiography, Reeve says he and his staff recognize that the intimate duties they must perform for him are a personal invasion and an indignity. He has finally come to accept this but says "I used to have to control my anger with myself for having ended up in this situation. Often I listen to music or watch TV so I don't have to think of being taken care of like a baby."

The family has no privacy. Reeve cannot be left alone for a moment, in case some of his life-support equipment should fail. He and his wife sleep alone but a monitor keeps a nearby nurse informed. Dana Reeve admits that she has sometimes turned the volume off on the monitor so that she and Reeve can discuss family matters and their own feelings in private. When he sleeps, Reeve always dreams that he is well. He has never had a dream in which he was paralyzed. He told Ann Curry of the "Today" show he believes he dreams he's not paralyzed because the essence of his being is still all in one piece.

Reeve's medical problems are numerous. His injury has blocked his ability to perspire, so summer heat could kill him. Within the 1997–1998 year, he was hospitalized eleven times for blood clots, pneumonia, high blood pressure, a collapsed lung, and an infection that nearly caused amputation of his leg. If he sits too long in any one position, circulation problems develop. A team massages him to stimulate circulation and rolls him over to examine his back for bedsores. "I'm thinking about charging admission," he joked with Walters. Because he cannot cough, his lungs must be cleared at regular intervals. A blockage of the bowels or the urinary tract is a constant threat; because he cannot feel, he cannot detect these conditions. Yet they could lead to a heart attack and death.

Dana Reeve explained to Walters that if Reeve could have one arm useful and active, he could wheel himself into the driveway, get into the van, and drive away all by himself. Stressing the difference that would make in their lives, she said, "One arm. That's all it would take."

While she has been instrumental in Reeve's care, Dana quickly denies the title some would give her—Saint Dana. She misses, she says, the small gestures of affection—holding hands, having him ruffle her hair—and she gets angry at the

Both Dana and Christopher Reeve have had their difficulties in coming to terms with the accident, but are committed to his recovery.

injustice of his injury. Asked if she tells Reeve, she replied that of course she does. He is her partner, her buddy, and the person with whom she shares everything. Both admit that they have arguments. But Reeve feels that his wife basically gave up 1995 and 1996 to take care of him, and since then it's been his responsibility to see that she got her life back. She has begun singing again in cabaret performances, played in an off-Broadway production, and she sang in a TV special designed to raise funds for spinal cord research.

Reeve is still interested in sports, though now he sails as a passenger instead of as skipper. But he says even if he can't play ball with his kids, he can give their athletic endeavors his undivided attention—something he might not have done before the accident. Will, at five, is a soccer enthusiast, and his father is his coach. The two older children have a more intellectual relationship with their father, and the "20/20" interview showed Reeve and his older son at a chess match, with his daughter making the moves Reeve called for.

THE PUBLIC CHRISTOPHER REEVE

Reeve has begun to work again. He narrated an animated feature, *The Quest for Camelot*, appeared in *Snakes and Ladders*, a movie about a paralyzed boy, and narrated *Without Pity*, an

Reeve with wife Dana and daughter Alexandra at the premiere of In the Gloaming, *a cable television movie that Reeve directed.*

HBO documentary. Reeve also directed a film for television called *In the Gloaming*, about a young man who returns to his family to die of AIDS. This film received a lot of praise and won four Cable Ace awards, and Reeve was nominated for an Emmy award. In September 1997, he flew to Atlanta to open the 10th Paralympic Games for 3,500 disabled contestants. On April 15, 1997, he was on Hollywood's Walk of Fame to receive his own star. He told the audience that he would return to stand by his star.

He now gets regular film offers, but he says the project has to be worthwhile before he will take it because any work takes such a toll on his energy. One offer he accepted had him playing the wheelchair-bound observer in a television version of Alfred Hitchcock's classic thriller, *Rear Window*, a role for which he won a Screen Actors Guild Award. In the spring of 2000, he directed a romantic film called *Heartbreaker*.

Reeve has also become one of the most sought-after motivational speakers in America, because his message is one of hope. He now earns a speaker's fee of $60,000, similar to that paid to former presidents. But such speeches are not easy for him. Travel requires that he ride in his customized van to the airport, accompanied not only by Dana but also by a team of assistants and medical aides. He must be transferred from his regular chair to a narrow one that will fit through the doorway of an airplane—usually one donated by the group that has hired him to speak. Before he boards the aircraft, his medical team massages his muscles to prevent in-flight spasms.

Reeve's autobiography, *Still Me*, earned him a reported $3-million advance and sold rapidly once

Reeve exiting his customized van to attend an event

it was on bookstore shelves. The title not only echoes the words Dana Reeve said to her husband when he first awakened from his coma but has a second meaning: Reeve is still, in the sense that he cannot move.

Still Me was written without the aid of another writer and critics have praised the book for its honesty and its lack of self-pity. The book reinforces Reeve's concern about funding and research on spinal cord injury, but most of it is devoted to describing his new existence. He is, wrote Jeff Guinn of the *Fort Worth Star-Telegram,* brave enough not to leave anything out, even the indignity of needing two people to put his underpants on for him. "*Still Me* should be required reading for anyone who feels sorry for himself," concluded Guinn.

When the book was released, Reeve made a flurry of appearances on such TV shows as "20/20," "The Oprah Winfrey Show," "Today," and "Larry King Live." Each time he appeared onstage, audiences went wild with applause. And live, on camera, Reeve still has the intensity he showed as Superman: his eyes sparkle with humor and sometimes mischief. When a young man on Winfrey's show, also a paraplegic, read the letter he'd written Reeve, one could see the emotion in the actor's eyes as he listened.

Do Reeve and his wife believe there is a reason for what has happened to their lives? Not at all. Reeve explains it as random, and Dana says it was an act of nature. "But God," she says, "comes in with the rush of people who come to help." And Reeve believes that it is what you do after a tragedy that gives the event meaning. Neither Reeve nor his wife indulge in "What if" thoughts. He has, he says, moved beyond that.

Do they think he will walk again? Reeve is determined that he will. His spinal cord has not been severed, as was originally thought, and he has sensation to the bottom of his spine. Reeve regularly exercises on a cycle that electrically

Reeve speaks with talk show host Larry King.

stimulates his muscles as he pedals. As a result, he has regained some feeling in his back and his left leg, according to interviewer Ivor Davis. He has motor skills, but his brain cannot communicate with his muscles and nerves. There is a gap of about 1⅛ inches (28 millimeters) in his spinal cord, and the small size of that gap makes him a candidate to walk again. Reeve focuses on recent research indicating that scientists are close to reconnecting the brain to paralyzed limbs. His vow to walk again is made more believable by the fact that he does walk about 3 or 4 miles (4.8 to 6.5 km) once a week for an hour, held up by harnesses and on a treadmill. The fact that he took steps, he says—and scientists agree—indicates that the spinal cord has memory. It remembers how to walk and could teach the legs the action again.

Reeve is convinced he will walk by the time he's fifty years old—in 2002. At a medical conference titled "A Look into the Future: Prospects for Treatment in the Year 2005," he told participants, "I'm glad you picked the year 2005, because I won't be here then. I'll be out sailing in Maine someplace." When asked if he didn't think he was naive to believe that he would walk again, he borrowed a page from one of his heroes, President John F. Kennedy. "He didn't say, 'We're going to go three-quarters of the way to the moon,'" Reeve said.

Dana is no less hopeful, but she is afraid to count on too much. She is, she says, sure that her husband will gain further use of his body, but she won't think about walking. It makes her afraid to hope for so much.

Ever the actor, Reeve constantly thinks about taking his first public steps and wants it to be something dramatic, in what he calls P. T. Barnum's style. "Where should we do it?" he asked Barbara Walters. "Should we rent Radio City?" He has also thought about the Academy Awards presentations since he astonished everyone by rolling onstage in his wheelchair in 1996. Maybe, he suggests, one day he could roll onstage in the chair and then, dramatically, stand up and walk. "It's fun to play with the idea," he says boyishly.

Once, in his Superman days, Reeve was asked his definition of a hero. He recalls saying that it was someone who commits a courageous act without considering the consequences. Now, he thinks a hero is the ordinary individual who finds the strength to endure.

CHRONOLOGY

1952   Christopher Reeve is born in New York City on September 25.

1953   Brother Benjamin is born; they are often called Tophy and Benjy.

1956   His parents divorce. Christopher and his brother, Benjamin, move to Princeton, New Jersey, with their mother, Barbara.

1959   Barbara Reeve marries Tristam Johnson in Princeton.

1962   Reeve's first stage performance, singing in a performance of Gilbert and Sullivan's *The Yeoman of the Guard*.

1968   Reeve is an apprentice at the Williamstown (Massachusetts) Theatre Festival.

1969   Performs in Turgenev's *A Month in the Country* at the Loeb Drama Center in Cambridge, Massachusetts, and at Maine's Boothbay Playhouse and the San Diego Shakespeare Festival.

1970   Reeve enrolls in Cornell College at Ithaca, New York.

1973	Reeve is accepted for drama instruction at the Juilliard School in New York City.
1974	Reeve earns a B.A. in English and music from Cornell University.
1975	Begins playing in TV soap opera, *Love of Life*.
1975	Performs in first Broadway role, playing opposite Katharine Hepburn in *A Matter of Gravity*.
1976	Gets first feature film role in *Gray Lady Down*.
1977	Reeve is chosen for the role of Superman
1978	*Superman, the Movie* is a box-office success; Reeve meets British model Gae Exton
1979	Reeve earns British Academy's Best Actor Award; first child, Matthew, is born to Gae Exton.
1980	Stars in *Superman II*.
1983	Stars in *Superman III*, with Richard Pryor.
1984	Daughter, Alexandra, is born; Reeve receives Circle K Humanitarian Award
1986	Works on first political campaign, for Vermont Senator Patrick Leahy, on environmental issues.
1987	Stars in *Superman IV*; relationship with Exton ends; Reeve meets and falls in love with Dana Morosini; travels to Chile to seek clemency for authors and playwrights sentenced to death under the regime of dictator Pinochet.
1988	The Walter Briehl Human Rights Foundation recognizes Reeve for bravery in Chile.
1990	Narrates TV documentary, *Black Tide*; lobbies in Washington for Clean Air Act

	Amendments and for preservation of the National Endowment for the Arts; tours the United States raising funds for AIDS victims; co-founds The Creative Coalition.
1992	Marries Dana Morosini; their son, Will, is born.
1995	Becomes quadriplegic after fall in precision horsemanship competition; begins intensive therapy; attends benefit dinner for Robin Williams; leaves rehabilitation center to go home and continue therapy
1996	Appears at 68th Annual Academy Awards ceremony; campaigns in Washington, D.C., for research funding for spinal-cord injury; becomes nationally sought motivational speaker on physical disabilities; is cast as voice of King Arthur in the animated cartoon, *Quest for Camelot*; first film-directing job *In the Gloaming;* appears at National Democratic Convention; the Christopher Reeve Foundation is established.
	Publishes autobiography/memoir, *Still Me,* and makes public appearances to promote the book.
1999	The Christopher Reeve Foundation and the American Paralysis Association merge to become the Christopher Reeve Paralysis Foundation; New York Governor George Pataki appoints Reeve to his state's Spinal Cord Injury Research Board; delivers commencement speech at the graduation ceremony at Williams College in Williamstown.

FILMOGRAPHY

Village of the Damned	1995
Speechless	1994
Above Suspicion	1995
Remains of the Day	1993
Noises Off	1992
Morning Glory	1993
Switching Channels	1988
Superman IV: The Quest for Peace	1987
Street Smart	1987
The Aviator	1985
The Bostonians	1984
Superman III	1983
Monsignor	1982
Deathtrap	1982
Superman II	1980
Superman, the Movie	1978
Gray Lady Down	1977

A NOTE ON SOURCES

Research about Christopher Reeve's life was made easier because his story is still unfolding. I began, as I always do, with a trip to the library, where I found two biographies, both of them several years old. They thoroughly covered Reeve's life before the accident.

Next I went to the web, where there are numerous Reeve sites. Some pages are hosted by fans as tributes—they can be helpful with lists of film and theater appearances, but the accuracy of information cannot be guaranteed. Other pages are research-oriented, some open fund-raising efforts for foundations devoted to spinal cord research. The web directed me, however, to major magazines carrying articles about Reeve—*Time*, *People*, *Parade*—and I went back to the library and the microfilm machines.

Finally, because Reeve's memoir, *Still Me*, was published while I was working on the biography, there were numerous short pieces in the newspapers about him, and he made many appearances on television programs such as the "Today" show. It was informative to listen to both Christopher and Dana talk and to watch their genuine smiles and affection for each other.

As for the Superman movies and the importance of Kryptonite, I had to ask my now-grown son, who gave me a thorough course in Superman mythology.

FOR MORE INFORMATION

BOOKS

Finn, Margaret L. *Christopher Reeve: Actor & Activist.* Chelsea House, 1997

Kosek, Jane K. *Learning about Courage from the Life of Christopher Reeve.* Rosen Publishing Group, 1999.

Reeve, Christopher. *Still Me.* Random House, 1998.

Reeve, Dana. *Care Packages: Letters to Christopher Reeve from Strangers and Other Friends.* Random House, 1999.

INTERNET SITES

Christopher Reeve Paralysis Foundation
http://www.apacure.com/
Learn more about spinal cord injury and current research programs to find a cure for paralysis.

Circle of Friends
http://www.circleoffriends.org
Established by Reeve and part of the Christopher Reeve Paralysis Foundation, this website offers message forums for paraplegics, quadriplegics, their families, and others. Also provides information on spinal cord injury.

Man of Steel
http://www.eonline.com/Hot/Features/Reeve
A lengthy interview with Reeve detailing his physical limitations and how he handles them

Movies of Christopher Reeve
http://www.imdb.com
Visit the Internet Movie Database site and conduct a search on Christopher Reeve to learn more about his many films and television appearances.

INDEX

ABOUT THE AUTHOR

Judy Alter saw *Superman, the Movie* with her then-young children over her protests that she wasn't interested in a comic-book hero. She was captivated by the film.

The author of fiction and nonfiction for readers of all ages, she lives in Fort Worth, Texas, where she is director of Texas Christian University Press. Her writing has won two Spur Awards from Western Writers of America, two Western Heritage (Wrangler) Awards from the National Cowboy Hall of Fame, and the Best Juvenile Novel of the Year award from the Texas Institute of Letters for *Luke and the Van Zandt County War*. Alter has written several books for Children's Press and Franklin Watts, including *The Santa Fe Trail* and *Women of the Old West*. Alter lives with two large dogs and two cats (left to her by her four now-grown children) and lists walking, cooking and reading as her hobbies